Written by John Bianchi
Illustrated by John Bianchi
Copyright 2001 by Pokeweed Press

Published by:
Pokeweed Press
Suite 337
829 Norwest Road
Kingston, Ontario
K7P 2N3

www.Pokeweed.com

Canadian Cataloguing in Publication Data

Bianchi, John
    Princess frownsalot

(Pokeweed Press new reader series)
ISBN 1-894323-28-9 (bound)   ISBN 1-894323-25-4 (pbk.)

    I. Title.

PS8553.I26P7 2001 jC813'.54   C2001-900102-9
PZ7.B47126Pr 2001

U.S. Cataloging-in-Publication Data
(Library of Congress standards)

Bianchi, John, 1947-
    Princess frownsalot / by John Bianchi. – 1st ed.
    [24] p. : col. ill. ; cm.
Originally published: Newburgh, Ont.: Bungalo Books, 1987.
Summary: An unpleasant princess has a frown stuck on her face and her
parents seek ways to remove it.
ISBN 1-894323-28-9 (library binding)
ISBN 1-894323-25-4 (pbk.)
1. Princesses – Fiction. 2. Happiness – Fiction. I. Title.
    [E] 21 2001   CIP   AC

Printed in Canada by:
Friesens Corporation

Canadian sales and marketing by:
General Publishing
895 Don Mills Rd.
400 – 2 Park Centre
Toronto, ON M3C 1W3

In Canada, order from:
General Distribution Services
325 Humber College Blvd.
Toronto, ON
M9W 7C3

Orders for Canada: 416-213-1919, ext. 199
Orders for U.S.A.: 1-800-805-1083

American sales and marketing by:
Stoddart Kids
a division of Stoddart Publishing Co. Ltd.
180 Varick Street, 9th Floor
New York, NY 10014

In the U.S.A., order from:
General Distribution Services
4500 Witmer Industrial Estates
Niagara Falls, NY
14092-1386

Available in the U.K. from:
Roundabout
31 Oakdale Glen
Harrogate HG1 2JY
England

Princess Frownsalot

By John Bianchi

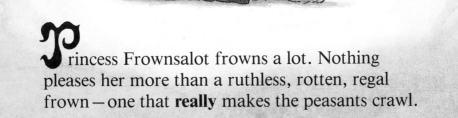

Princess Frownsalot frowns a lot. Nothing pleases her more than a ruthless, rotten, regal frown — one that **really** makes the peasants crawl.

Princess Frownsalot has the most feared frown in the entire kingdom. One frown from the castle balcony brings all her poor subjects to their knees.

Her highness always gets her way. She frowns her brother away
from the royal TV set. She frowns the King away from the last of
the chocolate chip cookies.

She frowns the Queen into reading her a bedtime story and then frowns the monsters out of her closet before she goes to sleep.

The reaction to her frowns always gives her and
her cat a really good laugh.

One day, while frowning some noisy little birds
away from the window ledge, a terrible thing
happens to Princess Frownsalot: her
frown . . . gets . . . stuck!

"HELP," exclaims the Princess, "I CAN'T UNFROWN MY FACE!" Her cat races to her mouth and tries to help. They both yank and twist and jerk and pry, but nothing can budge the frown.

"GET OFF ME YOU STUPID CAT!" screams the Princess. "GET THE QUEEN! GET THE KING!"

The King and Queen declare a national emergency. The great minds of the kingdom assemble before the Princess but **no one** can unfrown her face.

"GET THESE AIRHEADS AWAY FROM ME!" shouts Princess Frownsalot.

Finally, in a last-ditch attempt to save the Princess, the King and Queen decide to consult the greatest physician of the Dark Ages, Dr. Helmet von Katzinbottin.

"Vell, der is only vun solution," advises Dr. Katzinbottin, "I tink ve should go vid da transplant."

"**TRANSPLANT**?" echo the King and Queen and Princess.

"Ya. Ve try da schmile transplant."

Dr. Katzinbottin explains that a smile transplant is a complicated procedure. Finding the right donor could take some time.

"SO GET GOING!" screams Princess Frownsalot.

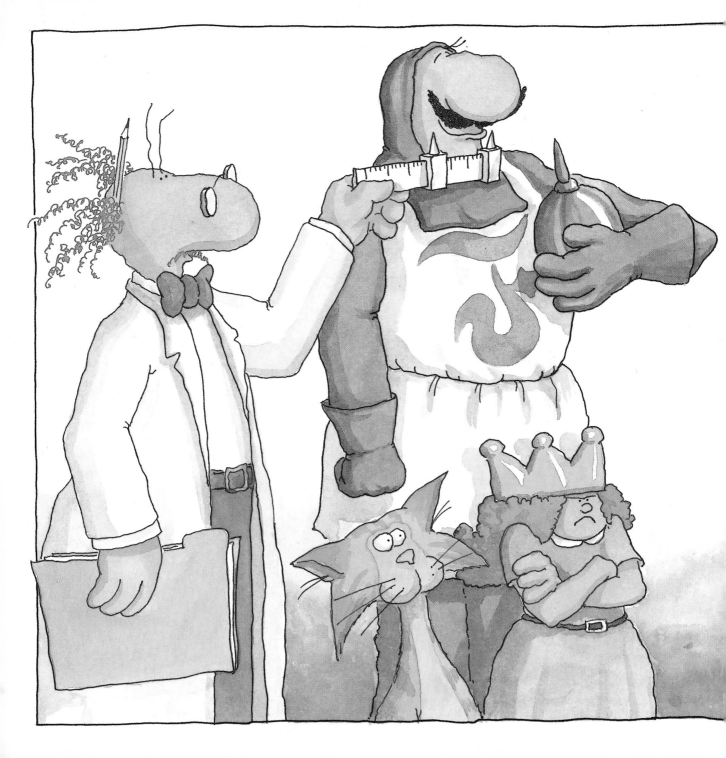

Dr. Katzinbottin launches a kingdom-wide search for the right smile. A senior medical student with an interest in art is called in to produce mock-ups of various smile combinations.

After two months, the Princess puts an abrupt end to Dr. Katzinbottin's smile search.

"I WANT MY TRANSPLANT NOW. **TODAY**!"

"But my majesty, our vork is not yet totally complete," replies the doctor.

"I WANT MY TRANSPLANT . . . THIS MINUTE!" screams the Princess. "WHO WILL BE MY DONOR?!"

In desperation, Dr. Helmut von Katzinbottin, points to the cat.

"Da . Da . . Da cat!" says the doctor,

"THE CAT?" asks the little princess.

"YA, da cat. Vhy not? He's got just da right schmile . . . "

The Princess's cat, who has been quite amused by the whole affair, suddenly changes his mood. In a blind panic, he makes a desperate dash for the door.

"SEIZE HIM!" shouts the Princess. "LET THE OPERATION BEGIN!"

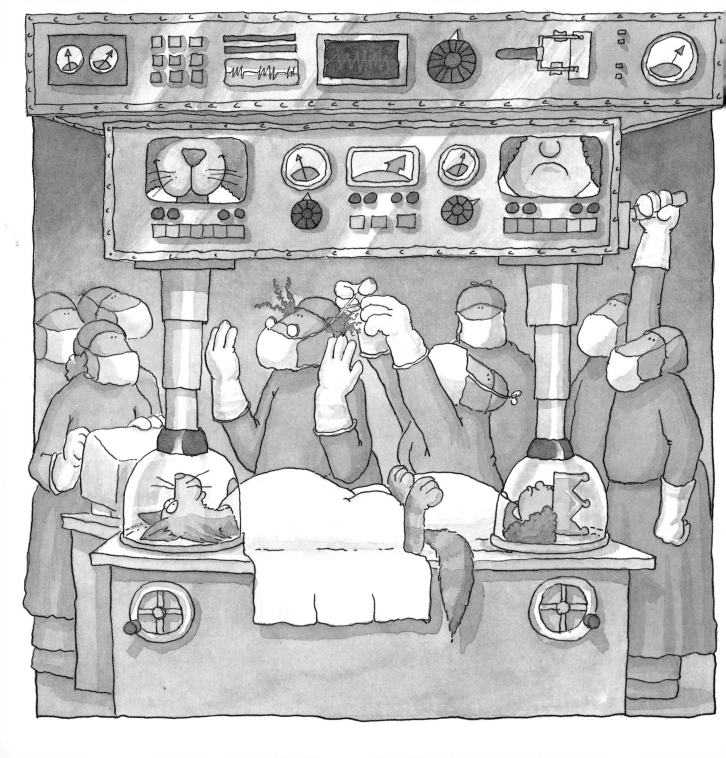

Princess Frownsalot and her cat are both placed under Dr. Katzinbottin's patented transplant machine. The extractor and implanter are carefully positioned.

A hush falls over the operating theatre as Dr. Katzinbottin strolls into the room. It has taken him many years of exhausting research and experimentation to develop this truly unbelievable technology. On the brink of medical history, Dr. Helmut von Katzinbottin pauses to reflect on those years of sacrifice and hardship . . . the first ever smile transplant will be his ultimate triumph.

"GET ON WITH IT, KETCHUP BOTTLES!" screams the little Princess.

The operation is a success. The doctor cautions the Princess that she must try to stay happy, or her face will reject the new smile. The Princess, muzzled in bandages, silently nods her head.

A few days later, the bandages removed, the Princess combs her hair.

"This smile isn't that bad," she thinks aloud. "I could have done without the whiskers though. What do you think, cat?

"Don't just sit there and frown. Cheer up. You're depressing me."

But the pathetic look on her kitty's face is too much for the Princess to bear. Overwhelmed with sadness, her new smile begins to droop.

"Oh, no," she says. "Rejection. What a waste of a good smile. You might as well have it back, cat."

After several minutes with a box of bandages, the smile and whiskers are back on the cat.

"At least you'll be able to smile," she says. "Those stupid whiskers never did much for me anyway."

This is the first time the Princess has given anything to anybody.

"Gee, that's funny," she thinks. "I feel . . . good."

The cat is elated. He bounces around the room and then gives the Princess a tremendous hug.

"Stop! Stop! STOP!" shouts the Princess. "YOU'RE TICKLING ME! YOU'RE TICKLING ME! YOU'RE EVEN MAKING ME LAUGH! AND IF I'M **LAUGHING**, I MUST BE **SMILING**!"

And sure enough, she was. And from then on, Princess Frownsalot was known as Princess Frownsalittle because she (and everybody around her) only frowned a little.

About the writer and illustrator . . .

John Bianchi was an avid artist from his earliest school days in Rochester, New York, entertaining his classmates with caricatures of the teachers and students around him. In his twenties, he became a full-time artist, selling his early work to tourists on the sidewalks of Ottawa. After a stint in an animation studio, he became a magazine illustrator.

He started illustrating and writing children's books in the mid-eighties and joined forces with editor Frank B. Edwards in 1986 to produce a long line of successful picture books that ranged from *The Bungalo Boys: Last of the Tree Ranchers* and *Princess Frownsalot* to *The Artist* and the *Pokeweed Public School* series. In 1999, he and Edwards launched Pokeweed Press as a vehicle to continue producing picture books that could be enjoyed by children and adults alike.

John works from a studio near Tucson, Arizona that offers views of the Sonoran Desert and the Catalina Mountains. He spends several weeks a year visiting schools to talk to students about his work as an artist and a writer.

You can write to John and Frank by email at:

mail@pokeweed.com

Teachers and students looking for resource material are welcome to visit:

WWW.POKEWEED.COM